DATE DUE

JE 19 '92	SEP. 1 9 1995	2 '06
	DEC 1 0 1996	
JY 21 '92	JY 10 97	Y 3 0 '06
SE 1 '92	AG 6 '97	10 '07
NOV 28 '92	AG 16 '97	AP 0 8 '13
FE 18 '93	AG 27 97	MY 0 7 '18
MR 11 '93	SE 8 97	MANOR 6-5-18
AP 15 '93	JA 11 '00	
MY 11 '93	FE 6 '00	
JE 14	NO 18 '00	
6-26-93	JA 21 2005	
MAY 22	AUG 2 8 201	

DEMCO

Thank you Caroline, Paul, Richard, Andrew, Chris (Mom), and Joan — Four Winds. Special thanks to Chris for all of it.

First published in the United States by
Ideals Publishing Corporation
Nashville, Tennessee 37214

First published in Great Britain by
Hutchinson Children's Books, an imprint of the
Random Century Group, Ltd.,
London, England

Text and illustrations copyright © 1990 Cliff Wright

ISBN 0-8249-8491-9

Printed and bound in Belgium

Designed by Paul Welti

Library of Congress Cataloging-in-Publication Data

Wright, Cliff.
   Crumbs! / Cliff Wright.
      p.   cm.
   Summary: To get an early taste of the cake made for his fifth birthday, Thomas dresses in a mouse costume, shrinks down, and joins a band of mice in their raid on the cake.
   ISBN 0-8249-8491-9
   [1. Mice—Fiction. 2. Size—Fiction. 3. Cake—Fiction. 4. Birthdays—Fiction.]   I. Title.
PZ7.W9347Cr   1990
[E]–dc20
                 90-5104
                 CIP
                 AC

CRUMB

E
WRI

S!

Cliff Wright

Ideals Children's Books · Nashville, Tennessee

Mom had just finished the surprise birthday cake for Thomas — chocolate, cherries and cream. She lit the candles for a moment and thought of how surprised he would be.

As she stepped to the sink, Thomas snuck into the kitchen and poked his fingers into the rich, drippy icing.

''Thomas!'' his mother cried. ''Take your fingers out at once!''

''Crumbs!'' muttered Thomas.

''Now go straight to your room,'' Mom said.

''But . . .'' said Thomas.

''No buts,'' Mom said, ''and you may not come down until I call you.''

Mom blew out the candles and put the glorious, gooey chocolate cake away in the pantry.

But small boys and chocolate cake are not easily parted.

There was something which Mom hadn't noticed. She had lit five candles in the cake. *Now there were only four . . .*

pitter-patter, pitter-patter

Scritch-scratch

rummage-scrummage   scribble-scrabble

CRUMBS!

Eeeek-squeak

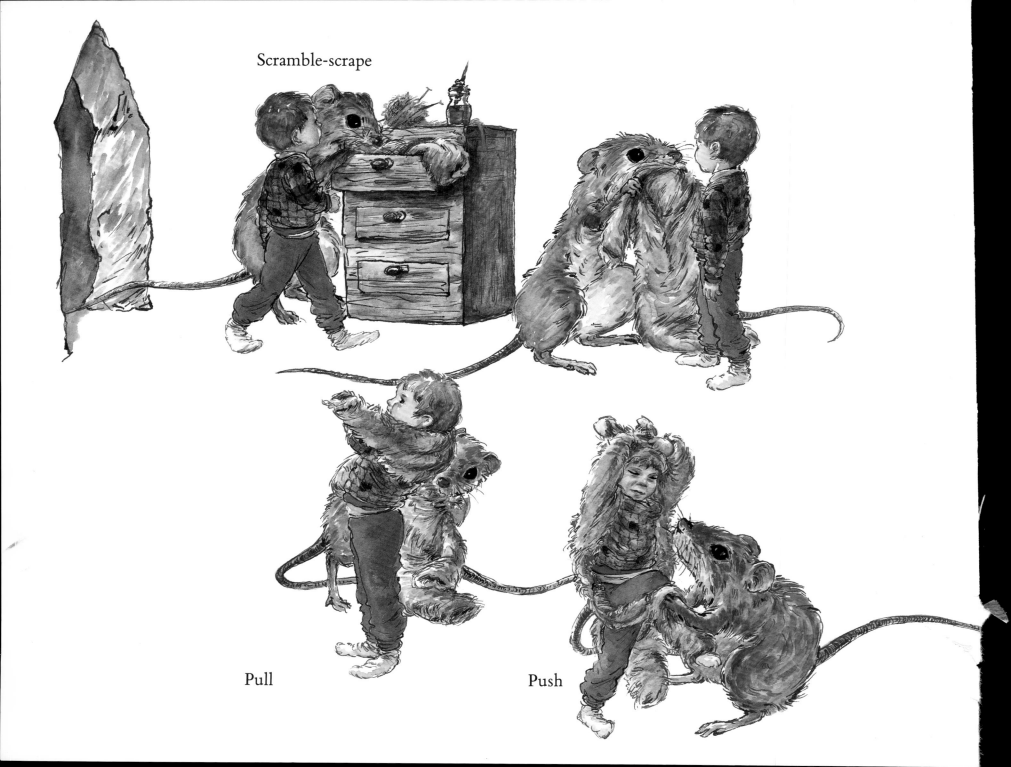

Scramble-scrape

Pull

Push

Swish-swosh

Slish-slosh

CRUMBS!

Skittle-scuttle

CRUMBS!

Oh, no!

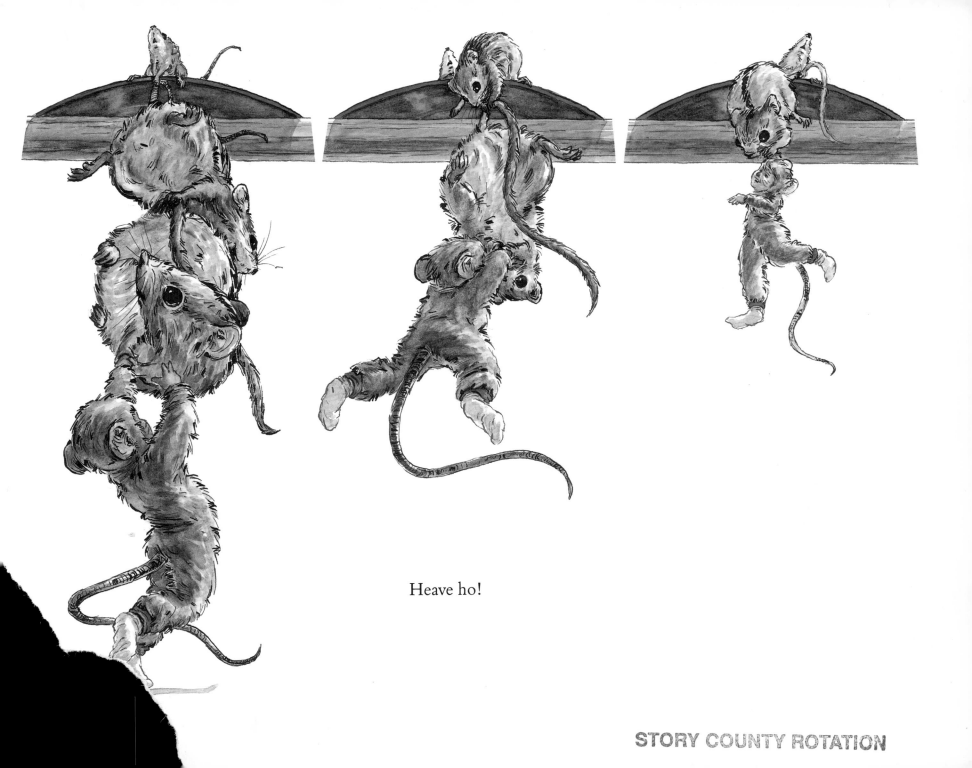

Heave ho!

CRUMBS!

Nibble-nibble
Chomp-chomp
Yum-yum
Yummy-yummy
Scrummy-scrummy

Mmmmmmmmmmmmmm . . .

Tick-tock, tick-tock, tick-tock,

tick-tock . . . four o'clock.

CRUMBS!

Creak-creak

Eeeek-eeek!

Shhh-shhh

"My cake!" cried Mom. "Now who on earth . . .
T-H-O-M-A-S!"

Wheeeeeeee

Bump!

Run-run-run-run-run!

Grumble-grumble,   rumble-rumble,   stomp-stomp,

Pitter-patter,   pitter-patter,   flurry-scurry,

stomp-stomp-stomp-stomp,　　　　　　　　　stomp

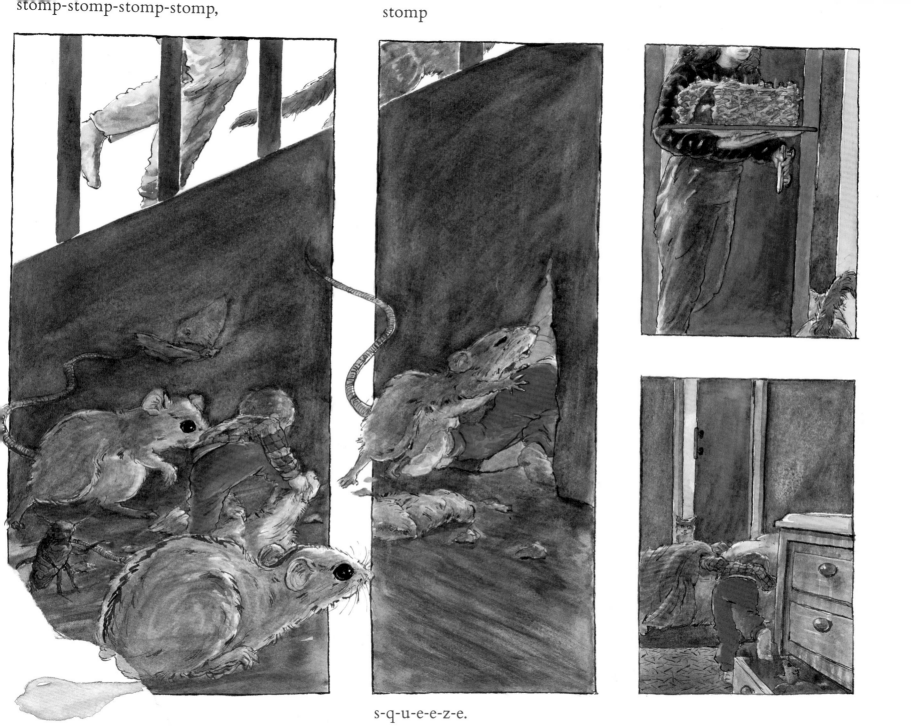

s-q-u-e-e-z-e.

Zzzzzzzzzzzzzz . . .   . . . zzzzzzzzzzzz   "Oh," said Mom, "he's fast asleep.

Well, that's funny. If it weren't Thomas, then . . .   CRUMBS! We must have . . .

mice!''

PRINTED IN BELGIUM BY
proost
INTERNATIONAL BOOK PRODUCTION

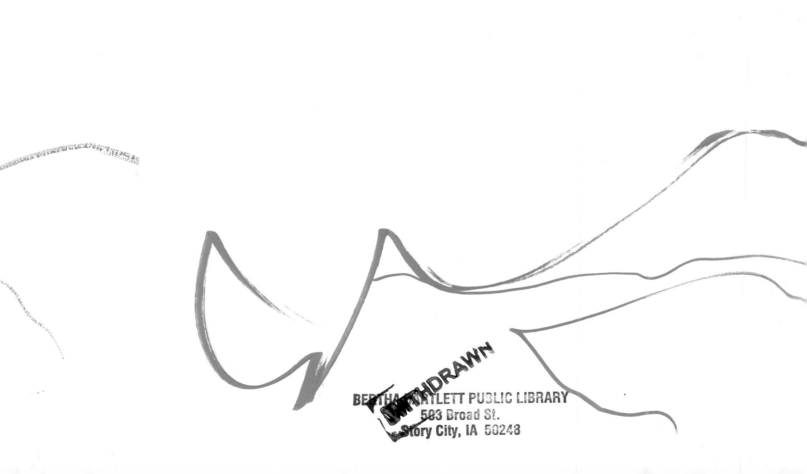